hoy Maties! Welcome aboard
the Great Adventures Pirate Ship.
Gather 'round to hear the story of
Ol' Bucky's treasure.

It was cleaning day. All the pirates
were hard at work polishing the brass
instruments, mending sails, and
repairing planks. All the pirates, that
is, except the lazy Scruffton, who was
in the crow's nest hidden by sails.

Scruffton might have gone unnoticed for the whole day, if his crow hadn't squawked and given him away. "Aha, you slacker," said Cap'n Doubloon. "Get down here and swab the deck."

Arggh," muttered Scruffton. "Some pirates have parrots.
I get a tattletale crow!"

"Squawk!" squawked the crow, as he landed on Scruffton's bucket
of soapy water.

Meanwhile, Barnacle Bob was scraping the outside of the ship when something caught his eye. He reached down and plucked a bottle from the sea. He pulled out the cork and took a note out of the bottle. "Cap'n Doubloon, look what I found!" Barnacle Bob exclaimed.

This be a treasure map," gasped the captain. "All hands on deck!" The crew crowded around for a peek.

The Demon Isle-33 leagues
NW of Pirate Island

This map will lead ye to my lair
And all the treasure hiding there.
Yet perils you will face, my friend,
Before your quest is at an end.
Your first step is to find the key.
'Tis gold and in pieces three.

aunted
ills

Treasure
Island

"Who is Ol' Bucky?" asked Barnacle Bob.

"Buck O'Neer," replied the captain. "One of the cleverest pirates ever to fly the Jolly Roger. He sailed the world collecting treasure. Who can say what fortune lurks in his hideout!"

"Who can say *he* doesn't lurk in his hideout," shuddered Barnacle Bob.

Cap'n Doubloon continued, "Legend has it that his ship went down to the briny deep in a monsoon. Maybe this map is all that survived the wreck."

Scruffton spoke up, "We're not far from Pirate Island. You can see it through the telescope."

"To your stations," called Cap'n Doubloon. "Treasure ho!"

As the ship neared Pirate Island, Scruffton said, "Look at that palm tree. That's the biggest coconut I've ever seen!"

"Coconut?" said the captain. "That be a cannonball!" As he spoke, a cannonball splashed into the sea, just missing the ship.

"This be one of Bucky's tests. Quick! On to Demon Isle!" the captain ordered.

When the crew reached Demon Isle, they dropped anchor. Cap'n Doubloon looked up from the map and said, "Bucky's map says we should head up the Rapid River, but it be too narrow for our ship. We'll have to travel in the dinghy. Scruffton and Barnacle Bob will join me."

As the pirates lowered the dinghy, the crow flew down from the mast and landed on Scruffton's shoulder.

"Shoo, bird," said Scruffton. But the crow wouldn't budge.

"A crow may bring us good luck, Scruffton," laughed Cap'n Doubloon.

ut instead of good luck, they found a waterfall. By the time they heard its roar, the boat had nearly tipped over the falls. Scruffton fired a hook into a grove of trees, and the boat held steady. But then the trees began to bend. Snap! The hook broke free, and the dinghy tumbled over the waterfall, breaking to bits.

Cap'n Doubloon and Scruffton came up splashing in the lake below the waterfall. But where was Barnacle Bob? They heard a faint cry, "Behind the waterfall. I found a cave." The two sailors paddled to the cave and saw Barnacle Bob sitting on a ledge. He was holding up part of a key.

The captain said, "Now we have a piece of the key, but we lost the map." Just then, they heard a familiar squawk. The crow held the treasure map in its beak. The bird dropped the map into Scruffton's hands.

"Good work! You're mighty useful, after all," said Scruffton.

The three pirates followed the map through the spooky Haunted Hills and stopped at the Lava Lagoon, where they noticed a trail of tiny volcanoes. They gathered branches to make a path over the bubbling, boiling lava. The last volcano held a surprise inside—the second piece of the key.

Safely beyond the lava, the three moved cautiously through dangerous quicksand to arrive at the Buggy Dunes, which were swarming with every imaginable kind of insect. "Just step lively and keep moving," ordered the captain. In the center of the dunes were two enormous skeletons connected by a huge spider web. Dangling from the top of the web was the final piece of the key.

"Cap'n, I'm used to climbing the ropes to the crow's nest. I can get the key," declared Scruffton.

"Climb away, mate," said the captain. "We'll keep an eye out for any eight-legged baddies."

Scruffton quickly scaled the spider web, carrying a knife in his mouth to cut down the key. As he neared the top, a giant black spider appeared. "It's guarding the key!" shouted the panicky Scruffton.

"Squawk," squawked the crow. The bird flew around the spider's head, and as the spider looked up, Scruffton raced up the web and cut down the key. "I got it!" he yelled. But now he was stuck in the sticky web. He cut away the web that trapped him and jumped. Pieces of web that clung to him billowed into a parachute and floated him gently to the ground.

"Thanks for the help, crow. Let's get out of here!" said the exhausted Scruffton.

The pirates scrambled out of the dunes and put the three pieces of the key together. They made a perfect fit! Then the three pirates followed the map to a wooden door in the side of a mountain. The captain put the key into the keyhole and turned it. The door groaned open to reveal Ol' Bucky sitting on a mound of jewels and gold coins!

"Hello," said Ol' Bucky, "I was hoping someone would come to visit. I was stranded here on Demon Isle when my ship sank. Hoarding treasure gets a wee bit lonely, so I sent out my map in a bottle."